BY
KIMBERLEE GARD

ILLUSTRATIONS BY
VIVIAN MINEKER

SNOOZA PALOOZA

To the yawners and dozers,
the nappers and snorers,
and all the snoozapaloozers!
Sweet dreams!
—K.G.

Published by Familius LLC, www.familius.com
1254 Commerce Way, Sanger, CA 93657

Familius books are available at special discounts for bulk purchases,
whether for sales promotions or for family or corporate use. For more information,
contact Familius Sales at 559-876-2170 or email orders@familius.com.

Library of Congress Control Number: 2020938270

Print ISBN 9781641702553
Ebook ISBN 9781641703789
KF 9781641704021
FE 9781641704267

Printed in China

Edited by Kaylee Mason and Brooke Jorden
Cover and book design by Carlos Guerrero

10 9 8 7 6 5 4 3 2 1

First Edition

SNOOZA PALOOZA

FAMILIUS

A cold wind blows, and snow starts to fall.
Mouse hides in a den that's cozy and small.

1 Snuggling into a wee-sized heap,
begins snoring and drifts off to sleep.
He dozes and dreams, tucked out of sight,
A snoozapalooza all day and all night.

Snail crawls in, slipping under a leaf.
Sealed up in her shell, she falls fast asleep.

Now 2 Snuggling into a tiny heap,
are snoring—they're both sound asleep.
They doze and they dream, tucked out of sight,
A snoozapalooza all day and all night.

Mole tunnels up from under the ground.
He sneaks in quietly, settling down.

Now 3 Snuggling into a little heap,
are snoring—they're all sound asleep.
They doze and they dream, tucked out of sight,
A snoozapalooza all day and all night.

In from the cold comes weary Chipmunk,
Nuzzling into a soft, furry bunk.

Snuggling into a bigger heap,
Now 4 are snoring—they're all sound asleep.
They doze and they dream, tucked out of sight,
A snoozapalooza all day and all night.

Hedgehog whirls by, slip-sliding on ice,
Tumbling in where it's cozy and nice.

Snuggling into a growing heap,
Now 5 are snoring—they're all sound asleep.
They doze and they dream, tucked out of sight,
A snoozapalooza all day and all night.

Rabbit scurries in, piling on,
Settling down with a stretch and a yawn.

Now 6 Snuggling into a rising heap,
are snoring—they're all sound asleep.
They doze and they dream, tucked out of sight,
A snoozapalooza all day and all night.

Skunk walks on *tiptoe*, without a peep.
She closes her eyes and nods off to sleep.

Now 7 Snuggling into a mighty heap,
are snoring—they're all sound asleep.
They doze and they dream, tucked out of sight,
A snoozapalooza all day and all night.

A gust of wind whirls outside the den.
Fox's teeth chatter—his fur stands on end.

Snuggling into a grand-size heap,
Now 8 are snoring—they're all sound asleep.
They doze and they dream, tucked out of sight,
A snoozapalooza all day and all night.

Grumpy Badger bores into the hole
And cuddles in between Rabbit and Mole.

Now 9 Snuggling into a giant heap,
are snoring—they're all sound asleep.
They doze and they dream, tucked out of sight,
A snoozapalooza all day and all night.

Bear's cold and tired—he needs a rest.
He squeezes inside and joins the snoozefest.

Now **10** Snuggling into a massive heap,
are snoring—they're all sound asleep.
They doze and they dream, tucked out of sight,
A snoozapalooza all day and all night.

All snuggled up into the middle,
They snore and they snooze, from big to little.

They snore, and snore, and then snore some MORE . . .
It's a Zzzz sounding R O A R . . . Rattling clear 'cross the
floor . . . Rumbling right out the door . . .

The other wood creatures tremble in fear.
"WHAT'S THAT SOUND?" they yell as they cover their ears.

They look and search for the source of the ROARRRR,
Then gape at the monstrous 10-ANIMAL SNORE!!!

Wren has an idea and begins to sing,
"Tweet-a-tweet" through the woods her tiny voice rings.

Robin joins the song—and then Chickadee.
Deer nods and hums loudly with Wild Turkey.

Elk bawls and Crow caws, while Moose snorts off-key.
Wolf howls and Squirrel chatters along noisily.

The 10-voice chorus, with sounds high and low,
Sings above the snores, and their rowdy song goes . . .

"Wake up! Wake up! Wake up!"
Mouse opens an eye as light fills the den,
He stretches and yawns with his other   friends!

Their long nap is done, but they make a pact:
"Next winter, we promise we'll all come back!"

And you can COUNT on that!